MW00875530

ISBN (Paperback): 979-8-9881073-1-6
ISBN (eBook): 979-8-9881073-0-9

This book is dedicated to my babies,
who are loved unconditionally.

Mom

Thank you to All who love me,
especially when I needed it most.

The porcupine was on his way to school when he met someone new.

"Hi, I'm Christopher. What's your name?" he said.

The skunk said, "I'm Rose, don't get close; I'm stinky."

He said, "Oh, I'm prickly. We can walk together."

On the way, they meet the raccoon.

Christopher said, "Hi Lucas, meet my new friend."

"What is that smell? Ugh," said the raccoon.

"Sorry, it's me," said the skunk.

Then they kept walking.

They stopped.

"Hi, I'm Ellie. We are having a snack. Do you want some nuts?" asked the squirrel. And then said, "This is Eddy."

The rooster looked at them; he did not want to share.

"No, thank you," they said.

They meet more others.

"Watch out; they'll hurt you," said Michael the fox.

"Welcome to the wood," said Katie,
the friendly bunny.

"I'm Alex," said the little deer.
"We're going to play ball."

At the wood ground, the others were playing kickball.

Christopher told Rose, "Do not get close; they don't let me play with them."

She asked, "Why not?"

The porcupine said, "Because I will hurt them with my quills."

The porcupine and skunk watched the others hug at the end of the game.

Christopher was sad and said, "It's OK, Rose, we don't need to play with them."

"We will do something about this," said Rose.

That night, the porcupine told his father, "Pop, I want to play with the others and hug them too."

His father said, "Oh, Christopher, you can't do that. Buddy, don't get close because you will hurt them. Please, stay away from others."

The porcupine went to his room sad.

That night Christopher dreamed about playing ball and being on the team.

They saw the Wise Owl on the way to school. "Who...Who...is this?" he asked.

"This is Rose; she's my best friend," said Christopher.

"Why the sad face?" asked the Owl.

They told him they could not play with the others because the porcupine was prickly and the skunk was smelly.

"Meet me by the fruit trees," he said.

They met the Owl, where there were blueberries and apple trees.

"Stay still, Christopher," and the bird flew over him.

The Owl put blueberries on the porcupine and said, "Maybe this will help, and you can get close to others."

"Yay, let's try it out!" said Rose.

When she went to hug the porcupine and got close, the blueberries popped and fell off. They broke and made a mess.

Pop, Pop, Pop...

"Yuck," said Rose.

"We tried," said the porcupine.

The next day, the porcupine was under a tree sad and said, "Rose, I don't think we can ever play on a team."

Then something fell and hit him on the head. BOP!

"What is that?" asked Rose.

"Oops," said Elie, who was in the tree eating walnuts. "Sorry, Christopher."

"Hey, the nut is stuck on your quill. I have an idea," said Rose.

They went to the Wise Owl and showed him the walnut on the porcupine's head.

"Let's try something," said the Owl.

They met at the nut tree.

Ellie threw the walnuts down, and the Owl put them on the porcupine's quills.

Christopher could not hurt others because he was not sharp.

"Yay," said Rose, "let's go play."

Christopher and Rose went to the wood ground, and the others looked at him funny.

"I can't hurt you," said the porcupine.
The fox said, "You can play, but Rose can't."
Christopher was sad and said, "We must let Rose be on the team."

"But she is stinky," said the raccoon.

"I can't play if my friend can't," said the porcupine.

On the way home, they saw the Owl.

"Who...Who...made you sad?" asked the Owl.

"I can play on the team, but Rose can't because they said she smells," said Christopher.

"Hmm, I have an idea. Meet me at the school tomorrow," said the Owl.

The Wise Owl knew what to do.

While flying, he saw clothes with clothespins to hang them.

He knew how to help Rose.

The Owl met them at the school and said he would put clothespins on their noses.

"No way, that will not work," said the fox.

"How will we breathe?"

"From your mouth," said the Wise Owl.

"Ok," said Alex, the deer.

The Owl put clothespins on all their noses.

Christopher had walnut shells on his quills so he could not hurt others, and the others had clothespins on their noses, so they could not smell Rose.

They all played ball together.

The porcupine and skunk won the game!

"Yay, Christopher! Yay, Rose! We love you!"
cheered the others.

When it was time for hugs, they stood in line and hugged Christopher and Rose one at a time.

The porcupine and skunk were happy that they could all play, hug, and love one another.

I hope you enjoyed the book and that it encourages you to share love and chase dreams.

For more inspirational books in the series, visit: www.vatsanabooks.com

Printed in the USA
CPSIA information can be obtained
at www.ICGtesting.com
JSHW041540230923
48887JS00009BA/64